Child's Play
Text © 2019 R. J. Peralta
Illustrations © 2019 Blanca Millán
This edition © 2019 Cuento de Luz SL
Calle Claveles, 10 | Urb. Monteclaro | Pozuelo de Alarcón | 28223 | Madrid | Spain
www.cuentodeluz.com
Original title in Spanish: *Juego de niños*
English translation by Jon Brokenbrow
Printed in PRC by Shanghai Chenxi Printing Co., Ltd. August 2019, print number 1695-16
ISBN: 978-84-16733-76-7
All rights reserved

CUENTO
DE LUZ

This book is printed on **Stone Paper** with silver **Cradle to Cradle™** certification.

Cradle to Cradle™ is one of the most demanding ecological certification systems, awarded to products that have been conceived and designed in an ecologically intelligent way.

Cradle to Cradle™ recognizes that environmentally safe materials are used in the manufacturing of Stone Paper which have been designed for re-use after recycling. The use of less energy in a more efficient way, together with the fact that no water, trees nor bleach are required, were decisive factors in awarding this valuable certification.

To my parents, my brothers and sisters,
for all our trips together.
— R. J. Peralta —

To all the families that travel the world
with their homes in tow..
— Blanca Millán —

CHILD'S PLAY

R. J. Peralta   Blanca Millán

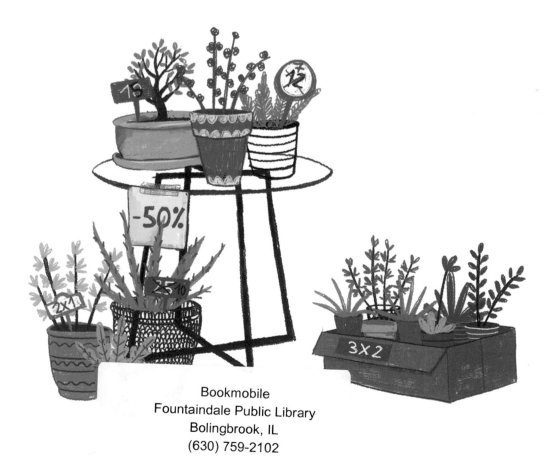

This is the story of Danny, who's a great singer.

He loves thinking up new songs, all about amazing places and futuristic cities, about people who lived in the past, or just everyday things.

Every time Danny has something to say, he sings it instead. Making music is what he does best.

His music helps him feel better when something goes wrong . . .

... and feel happy when there's something to celebrate.

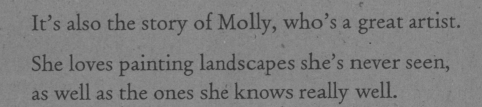

It's also the story of Molly, who's a great artist.

She loves painting landscapes she's never seen,
as well as the ones she knows really well.

Every time she feels an emotion welling up inside, she lets it out by painting or drawing. Making art is what she does best.

She loves her pencils and brushes, and the colors that burst from them, which are warm or cold, depending on the feeling she has deep inside.

And finally, it's the story of little Marcus,
who's a great writer.

He loves describing far-off kingdoms,
and tropical islands,
but also the experiences he has every day,
and the things his friends talk about.

Whenever he feels inspired, he starts writing.
Sometimes he writes poems, or tells stories, and
other times he just writes down the thoughts going
through his head.

He loves his pen and his pencil, and the notebooks
he fills with words, one after another; sad words,
happy words, and sometimes words that only make
sense to him.

Danny, Molly, and Marcus love being together. They love playing together, and inventing things together.

Stories with pictures and paintings, stories with songs and music.

Sometimes, without meaning to, they start singing, painting, and writing while they're in class, or in the middle of conversations or important meetings.

They can't help it: it's just the way they are.

When they hear loud noises, they become immersed in their own little worlds.

They're so, so focused, that they can't hear anything that comes from outside.
Only their own creations.

Their teachers are worried, because they
don't pay attention at school.

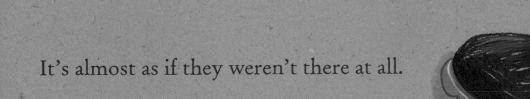

It's almost as if they weren't there at all.

Their parents don't always understand them.
They think they spend their days in their own
little worlds.

And sometimes, when they need quiet so they can think, or want to watch the news on the TV, then they tell them to stop making such a racket.

The three of them spend most of their mornings and evenings creating things. They often forget about everything else, even whether they've had dinner or not.

In their own little worlds, they're never
short of anything, especially love, love
of adventure, and good company.

Danny, Molly, and Marcus sometimes feel worried,
like at dinner time, or when their parents are angry.

But above all, they're worried about moving.
They will be going to live in a new house in a
new country in just a few days.

The guitar makes a horrible twanging sound; the colors are dark, and the lines are spiky; and the stories are scary. Every time they talk about the new house, and of course, the new school, and the new friends they'll have to make . . . everything is pretty frightening.

But one day, before they head off to their new home,
Danny tells them something he's heard in class.

"Home is where the heart is, and the family."

Then he tells them that the thing he loves
the most is writing his own songs.

Molly talks about her paintings and her drawings.

And Marcus talks about his books full of stories,
poems, and adventures.

They all love playing together and inventing
stories and worlds that are funny, amazing,
or terrifying.

The new house might not be the prettiest in the world, but as long as they're together and keep on singing, painting, writing, playing, and laughing, their home won't change even a little bit. Because home is wherever they can be together.